The YELLOW SUITCASE

story by Meera Sriram
pictures by Meera Sethi

penny
candy
BOOKS

Penny Candy Books
Oklahoma City & Savannah
Text © 2019 Meera Sriram
Illustrations & background textures © 2019 Meera Sethi

 This book is printed on paper certified to the environmental and social standards of the Forest Stewardship Council™ (FSC®).

Photo of Meera Sriram: Sriram Gopalakrishnan
Photo of Meera Sethi: Vivek Shraya
Design: Shanna Compton

23 22 21 20 19   1 2 3 4 5
ISBN-13: 978-0-9996584-1-3 (hardcover)

Small press. Big conversations.
www.pennycandybooks.com

For my husband and his mother.

Asha rested her head on the taxi window. People, houses, cows, markets, and vehicles passed by.

The city streets always bustled in India.

When the taxi pulled over, Asha looked past the palms and marigolds.

But Grandma wasn't waiting on the front porch.

The afternoon air was hot and still under a cloudless sky.

Asha followed her parents into her grandmother's house, the luggage tag swinging back and forth, as she wheeled her tiny, yellow suitcase along.

Inside, unfamiliar faces greeted Asha; familiar relatives talked about Grandma. The scent of jasmine flowers and incense smoke stung Asha's nose as she walked closer to Grandma's picture on a wall shelf.

"Where's Grandma?" Asha asked, even though she knew.

"She's not here. She's not anywhere." Dad wrapped his arms around Asha. "We talked about it. . . ."

Asha gripped the handle of her suitcase a bit tighter.

SWEET LADY

HAIR - PIN

SHIP

STAMP PAD

BEST QUALITY

WELCOME

PREMIUM

GREEN LABEL TEA

MANGO

SWEET x SALTY

PICKLE

Every summer she carried presents for Grandma in her bright yellow suitcase. And later packed it with gifts Grandma gave her to take back to California— wooden toys, comics, handmade dolls, spinning tops, coins, dresses, and sweets.

"Will I ever see her again?" Asha asked.

Dad sank into a chair saying nothing, and Asha saw him cry for the first time.

For the next several days, Mom and Dad mourned Grandma's passing with prayers and offerings. The relatives joined them.

But Asha kept to herself in the backyard. She sat on her suitcase putting stickers on it and making cards.

She watched sparrows and squirrels build homes and collect food. Sometimes, she read under the coconut tree.

"Are you OK, Asha?" Mom asked one afternoon.

Asha unzipped the suitcase and shook it. Little gift boxes, envelopes, and greeting cards scattered onto the floor.

"NO! I'm not OK!" She stomped into the bedroom with the empty suitcase and kicked it under the bed.

Mom followed quietly.

"Why *did* we bring this suitcase?" Asha yelled, crawling into bed.

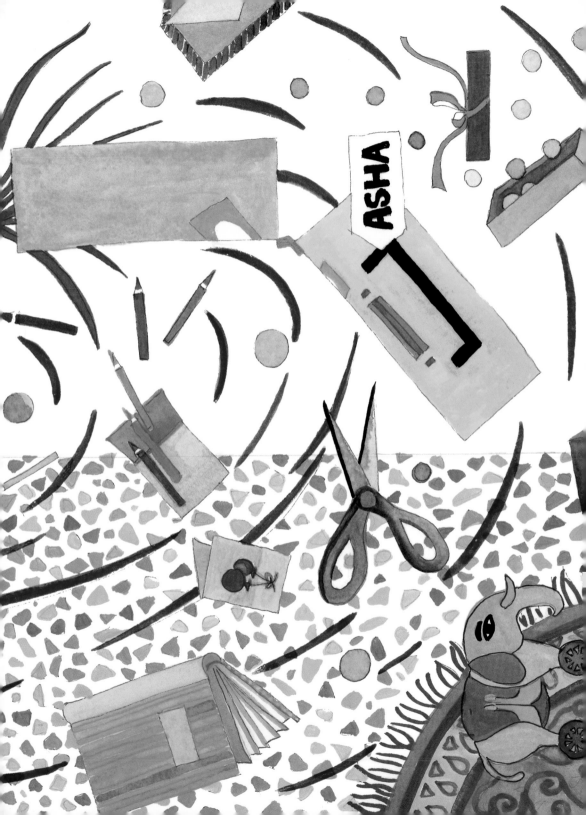

She missed the aroma of cardamom-spiced chai and of sweet ghee that filled the house when Grandma was around. And she missed the touch of the soft cotton saris Grandma wore.

"Maybe we should've been here earlier to save Grandma," Asha said.

"But that wouldn't have changed anything, dear," Mom said, stroking Asha's hair. "Grandma was very sick."

Asha pulled the blanket over her face.

At the end of two weeks, Dad packed their bags.

He pulled out the yellow suitcase from under the bed. "Aren't you going to take your suitcase with you, Asha?"

"It's empty, Dad!" Asha tossed the suitcase aside.

But the yellow suitcase popped open revealing a colorful quilt. Asha recognized the patches—rectangles of red paisleys and green leaves, and squares of blue flowers and maroon swirls—bits of Grandma's saris stitched together . . .

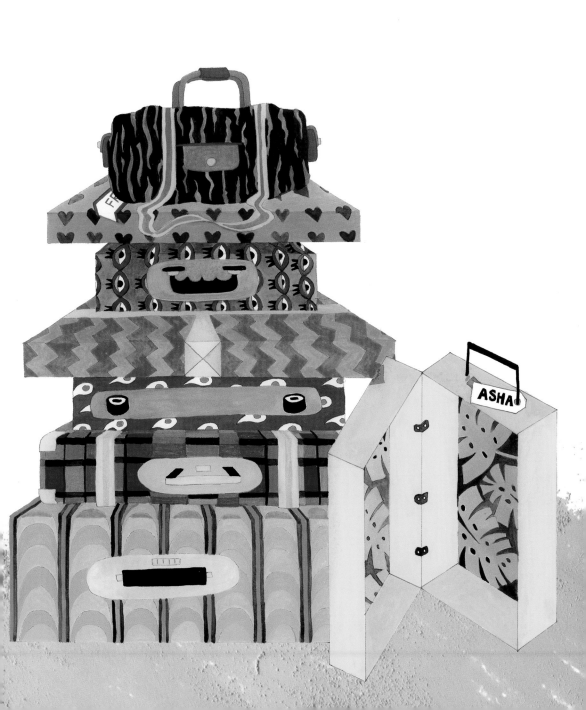

. . . she gathered the sari quilt in her arms. She could smell Grandma's talcum powder. She ran her fingertips over the threads that spelled her name.

Dad sat beside her. "Grandma was working on it until she left for the hospital."

Tears dripped down Asha's face and onto the yellow suitcase, like fat raindrops falling on a sunflower.

"I miss her too," Dad said and patted Asha's back.

The cab driver honked louder, and Dad walked out with his bags. Asha held on to her suitcase.

She tucked Grandma's picture between the folds of the sari quilt; she made a label and taped it close to the luggage tag.

"Hurry up, dear," Mom called.

Hugging her suitcase close, Asha glanced out the taxi window and smiled.

Grandma's marigolds swayed in the evening breeze as the taxi jostled its way to the airport on a narrow dirt road.

Author's Note

The Yellow Suitcase was inspired by my own family's experience, when my children lost their first grandparent in India in the spring of 2010. The thirty-two-hour journey from California to India, burdened with mixed emotions, was harrowing. Growing up in the US my children were not exposed to funeral customs in India. They were uncomfortable and scared, while still going through all the stages of grief—denial, anger, guilt, sadness, and acceptance—to cope with the loss, just like we did.

MEERA SRIRAM grew up in India and moved to the US at the turn of the millennium. An electrical engineer in her past life, she now enjoys writing for children and advocating early and multicultural literacy. Meera has coauthored several books published in India. She believes in the transformative power of stories and writes on cross-cultural experiences that often take her back to her roots. Meera loves yoga and chai, and lives with her husband and two children in Berkeley, California, where she fantasizes about a world with no borders.

MEERA SETHI was born in New Delhi, India and immigrated to Toronto, Canada as a child. She has spent her life traveling back and forth between these two countries, a journey that has deeply inspired her art. Today, Meera lives and works in Toronto as an artist immersed in stories of diaspora, belonging, and the self as woven through the textile, clothing, and fashion. Her work has been featured in NBC, NPR, the *Toronto Star,* the *Globe and Mail*, the *Fader*, *Vice*, *Vogue India*, *CNN*, *MTV,* and numerous other print and online publications. *The Yellow Suitcase* is her first picture book.